SUCCESSORIES®

# Great Quotes from Zig Ziglar

SUCCESSORIES®

# Great Quotes from Zig Ziglar

CAREER PRESS
3 Tice Road, P.O. Box 687
Franklin Lakes, NJ  07417
1-800-CAREER-1
201-848-0310 (NJ and outside U.S.)
FAX: 201-848-1727

**SUCCESSORIES: GREAT QUOTES FROM ZIG ZIGLAR**
Cover design by The Hub Graphics Corp.
Printed in the U.S.A. by Book-mart Press

To order this title, please call toll-free 1-800-CAREER-1 (NJ and
Canada: 201-848-0310) to order using VISA or MasterCard, or for
further information on books from Career Press.

**Library of Congress Cataloging-in-Publication Data**

Ziglar, Zig.
    Great quotes from Zig Ziglar.
        p. cm.--(Successories)
    ISBN 1-56414-289-2
1. Quotations, English. I. Title. II. Series.
    PN6081.Z54        1997
    158'DC21                                              98-51682
                                                              CIP

# DEDICATION

This book is dedicated to those who have a zest for life, a thirst for knowledge, a need to achieve or a desire to excel. It's written to those who want to learn from the past, to more thoroughly enjoy the present and to more adequately prepare for the future. Some of the quotes are my own, some are from famous and not-so-famous people, and some are familiar sayings of unknown origin. They were selected for the purpose of raising sights, changing lives and giving encouragement to those who seek a revitalization of their thinking, a reassessment of their values and a challenge to be all they can be so they can make their mark in today's demanding world.

SEE YOU AT THE TOP!

*Zig Ziglar*

# CONTENTS

You can have
everything in life you
want, if you will just
help enough other
people get what they
want.

—Zig Ziglar

When you change your attitude
about your job, it'll make a
dramatic difference about your
performance on the job.


Being cheerful keeps you healthy.
—King Solomon


If you go out looking for friends,
you're going to find they're very
scarce. If you go out to be a friend,
you'll find them everywhere.

# ATTITUDE

Ask yourself a question: Is my attitude worth catching?

You never work for somebody else. Someone else might sign your check, but you're the one who fills in the amount.

It's your attitude and not your aptitude that determines your altitude.

# ATTITUDE

You cannot tailor-make the
situations in life, but you can
tailor-make the attitudes to fit
those situations.

Discouraged? Just remember that
the darkest night did not turn out all
the stars.

What happens to a man is less
significant than what happens
within him.
—Louis L. Mann

# ATTITUDE

How you get up in the morning will play a big part in how high you go up in life.

If you learn from a defeat, you haven't really lost.

Remember that failure is an event—not a person.

# ATTITUDE

Today's fringe benefits are
tomorrow's expectations.

Your past is important, but it is not
nearly as important to your present
as is the way you see your future.
—Dr. Tony Campolo

If there's hope in the future there is
power in the present.
—John Maxwell

# ATTITUDE

I'm super good, but I'll get better.

You already have every
characteristic necessary for success.

Regardless of your past, your future
is a clean slate.

# Dale Carnegie

# ATTITUDE

Of all the things you wear, your expression is the most important.

—Janet Lane

Remember, happiness doesn't depend upon who you are or what you have; it depends solely upon what you think.

—Dale Carnegie,
author and lecturer

The surest way to knock the chip off a shoulder is a pat on the back.

# ATTITUDE

Whatever happens, do not lose hold of the two main ropes of life—hope and faith.

Don't be afraid of opposition. Remember, a kite rises against— not with—the wind.

—Hamilton Mabie

Expect the best. Prepare for the worst. Capitalize on what comes.

# ATTITUDE

When a happy person comes into the room, it is as if another candle has been lit.
—Ralph Waldo Emerson,
philosophical essayist, poet and lecturer

If things go wrong, don't go with them.
—Roger Babson

Happiness is not something you find, but rather something you create.

# ATTITUDE

Recognizing a problem doesn't always bring a solution, but until we recognize that problem, there can be no solution.

—James Baldwin,
novelist, essayist and playwright

Whether you think you can or think you can't—you are right.

—Henry Ford,
automobile production pioneer

Your attitude is more important than your aptitude.

# ATTITUDE

Winning is not everything, but
making the effort to win is.
—Vince Lombardi,
NFL coach

Every thought that goes into
your mind has an effect to some
degree.

Many times the difference between
your accomplishment and your
failure is your attitude.

# Norman V. Peale

# ATTITUDE

Your living is determined not so much by what life brings to you as by the attitude you bring to life; not so much by what happens to you as by the way your mind looks at what happens.

—John Homer Miller

Any fact facing us is not as important as our attitude toward it, for that determines our success or failure.

—Norman Vincent Peale,
philosopher and author

# ATTITUDE

It's not the situation... It's your reaction to the situation.

Others can stop you temporarily—you are the only one who can do it permanently.

—Zig Ziglar

There is nothing either good or bad, but thinking makes it so.

—William Shakespeare,
English playwright and poet

# Winners evaluate themselves in a positive manner and look for their strengths as they work to overcome weaknesses.

—Zig Ziglar

# SELF-IMAGE

A strong, positive self-image is the best possible preparation for success in life.
—Dr. Joyce Brothers,
psychologist

When your image improves, your performance improves.

When your confidence goes up, your competence goes up at the same time.

# SELF-IMAGE

You will make a lousy anybody else, but you are the best *you* in existence.

One reason people never attempt new things is their fear of failure.

Many times our weaknesses are extensions of our strengths.

# SELF-IMAGE

The biggest failure of all is the
person that never tries.
—Dr. Larry Kimsey

No one can make you feel inferior
without your consent
—Eleanor Roosevelt,
humanitarian, former first lady

Be not deceived, evil companions
corrupt good morals.
—1 Corinthians 15:33

# SELF-IMAGE

The starting point for both success
and happiness is a healthy
self-image.

The way you look on the outside
has a definite bearing on how you
feel and see yourself on the inside.

No one is useless in this world who
lightens the burden of it for
anyone else.
—Charles Dickens,
English author

# SELF-IMAGE

A sincere compliment is one of the most effective motivational methods in existence.

Success occurs when opportunity meets preparation.

You gotta be before you can do, and you've gotta do before you can have.

—Zig Ziglar

# SELF-IMAGE

Every job is a self-portrait of the person who did it.

Positive thinking is the hope that you can move mountains. Positive believing is the same hope but with a reason for believing you can do it.

A good, firm handshake is essential to the development of a personality.

## SELF-IMAGE

Once you have accepted yourself, it's so much easier to accept other people and their points of view.

Everyone, including you, just naturally feels better when exposed to a cheerful, optimistic individual, regardless of the nature or length of the contact.

To build your self-image, you need join the smile, firm handshake and compliment club.

# SELF-IMAGE

If you will set the example, you won't need to set many rules.
—Mama Ziglar

To build a healthy self-image, finish the job.

A healthy self-image is simply becoming the best "*you*" that you can possibly be.

Conceit is a weird disease. It makes everybody sick except the one who's got it.

What you get by reaching your destination isn't nearly as important as what you become by reaching that destination.

Opportunity lies in the man and not in the job.

# SELF-IMAGE

You cannot consistently perform in a manner which is inconsistent with the way you see yourself.
—Dr. Joyce Brothers, psychologist

You must begin to think of yourself as becoming the person you want to be.
—David Viscott

To improve your self-image, do something for someone else.

## SELF-IMAGE

Do not wish to be anything but what you are, and try to be that perfectly.

—St. Francis De Sales

Some people are so heavenly minded they're no earthly good.

Character may be manifested in the great moments, but it is made in the small ones.

—Phillips Brooks

If you do the things
you need to do when
you need to do them,
then someday you
can do the things you
want to do when you
want to do them.

—Zig Ziglar

# GOALS

Success consists of a series of little daily efforts.
—Mamie McCullough

People often complain about lack of time when the lack of direction is the real problem.

Go as far as you can see, and when you get there you will always be able to see farther.
—Zig Ziglar

# GOALS

Our daily objectives should include an honest effort to improve on yesterday.

The only way to reach your long-range goals is through achieving your short-range objectives.

You don't pay the price for success, you enjoy the benefits of success.
—Zig Ziglar

# GOALS

Give me a stock clerk with a goal,
and I will give you a man who will
make history. Give me a man
without a goal, and I will give you
a stock clerk.

—J. C. Penney,
department store magnate

You measure the size of the
acomplishment by the obstacles
you had to overcome to reach
your goals.

—Booker T. Washington,
educator

# Booker T. Washington

# GOALS

Outstanding people have one thing in common: an absolute sense of mission.

A goal properly set is halfway reached.

Effort is the key, but direction and loyalty are paramount.

# G O A L S

Desire is the great equalizer.

When you've got a solid
commitment and solid objectives,
you've got a much better chance of
reaching your goal.

You need to see yourself as already
being and achieving your objective.

# Helen Keller

# GOALS

When you're looking at the sun,
you see no shadows.

—Helen Keller,
author and lecturer

When the outlook isn't good, try
the uplook—it's always good.

When you learn how to set
one goal, you'll know how to
set all goals.

# GOALS

What you get by reaching your destination isn't nearly as important as what you become by reaching that destination.

A goal casually set and lightly taken is freely abandoned at the first obstacle.

Those who say it can't be done are usually interrupted by others doing it.

# GOALS

It's just as difficult to reach a destination you don't have, as it is to come back from a place you've never been.

This one step—choosing a goal and sticking to it—changes everything.
—Scott Reed

If you don't know where you are going, how can you expect to get there?
—Basil S. Walsh

# GOALS

If you take the train off the tracks, it's free but it can't go anywhere.

Obstacles are those frightful things you see when you take your eyes off your goals.

The most important thing about goals is having one.

—Geoffry F. Abert

# G O A L S

The indispensable first step to getting the things you want out of life is this: Decide what you want.
—Ben Stein

Every choice has an end result.

In whatever position you find yourself, determine first your objective.
—Ferdinand Foch,
French army marshal

# GOALS

If a man knows not what harbor he seeks, any wind is the right wind.
—Seneca, Roman writer,
philosopher and statesman

A man without a purpose is like a ship without a rudder.
—Thomas Carlyle,
Scottish historian and philosopher

Goals are dreams we convert to plans and take action to fulfil.
—Zig Ziglar

You are what you are
and where you are
because of what's
gone into your mind.
You can change what
you are and where
you are by changing
what goes into your
mind.

—Zig Ziglar

# MOTIVATION

The foundation stones for a
balanced success are honesty,
character, integrity, faith, love
and loyalty.

—Zig Ziglar

He who chooses the beginning of a
road, also chooses its outcome.

Ability may get you to the top, but
it takes character to keep you there.

—John Wooden,
NCAA coach

# MOTIVATION

It's not where you start but where you finish that counts.

You have within you all of the qualities necessary for success.

In your hands you hold the seeds of failure or the potential for greatness.

# MOTIVATION

Anyone who thinks they can go to the top and stay there without being honest, is dumb.

—Mortimer Feinberg

You need to accept the fact that from this moment on, your situation and future is in capable hands—yours.

There is power in words. What you say is what you get.

# MOTIVATION

A sincere compliment is one of the most effective tools to teach and motivate others.

The choices you make on a daily basis affect what you will have, be or do in the tomorrows of your life.

Anything worth doing is worth doing poorly, until you can learn to do it well.

—Steve Brown

# Abraham Lincoln

# MOTIVATION

Your natural resources, unlike the natural resources on planet Earth, will be wasted and "used up" only if they are never used at all.

If it is to be, it is up to me.

Keep trying. It's only from the valley that the mountain seems high.

# MOTIVATION

You cannot escape the
responsibility tomorrow by evading
it today.
—Abraham Lincoln,
16th president of the U.S.

When we change the input into our
minds, we change the output into
our lives.

We are free up to the point of
choice, then the choice controls
the chooser.
—Mary Crowley

# MOTIVATION

What lies behind us and what lies
before us are tiny matters
compared to what lies within us.
—Ralph Waldo Emerson, philosophical
essayist, poet and lecturer

The explanation of triumph is all in
the first syllable.

Your success and happiness
start with *you*.

# MOTIVATION

Don't get discouraged; it is often the last key in the bunch that opens the lock.

For the resolute and determined there is time and opportunity.
—Ralph Waldo Emerson, philosophical essayist, poet and lecturer

You can finish school; you can even make it easy. That's not true of education. You never finish it, and it is seldom easy.

# MOTIVATION

There is a loftier ambition than merely to stand high in the world. It is to stoop down and lift mankind a little higher.
—Henry Van Dyke

It's what you learn after you know it all that counts.

"I can't do it" never yet accomplished anything; "I will try" has performed wonders.
—George P. Burnham

# MOTIVATION

You are the only person on this earth who can use your ability.

You learn from successful failures.

Desire is the ingredient that changes the hot water of mediocrity to the steam of outstanding success.

# MOTIVATION

The difference between a big shot and a little shot is that a big shot's just a little shot that kept on shooting.

If you're in something, get in it. If you're not in it, get out.
—Mama Ziglar

I've got to say no to the good so I can say yes to the best.

# MOTIVATION

Imagination is the strongest nation on earth.

The way you get out of a job you don't like is to do it so extraordinarily well that nobody can afford to keep you in that position.

You may give out, but never give up.

—Mary Crowley

# MOTIVATION

Intelligent ignorance is the seed of hope, the promise of good in everything that happens to us.

Ability can take you to the top, but it takes character to keep you there.

There is always a demand for dedicated, enthusiastic workers.

# MOTIVATION

Nothing in the world can take the place of persistence. Talent will not. Nothing is more common than unsuccessful men with talent. Genius will not. Unrewarded genius is almost a proverb. Education will not. The world is full of educated derelicts. Persistence, determination and hard work make the difference.

—Calvin Coolidge,
30th president or the U.S.

When you do more than you're paid to do, you will eventually be paid more for what you do.

What you do off the
job determines how
far you will go on
the job.

—Zig Ziglar

Success comes when preparation meets opportunity.

Your yearning power is more important than your earning power.

By doing the best we can, we are winners, and the more experience we have at winning, the better we become at acquiring the characteristics of being good winners.

# SUCCESS

When we give it our all, we can live with ourselves—regardless of the results.

The true reward of a thing well done is to have done it.

Character is the ability to carry out a good resolution long after the excitement of the moment has passed.

—Cavett Robert

# SUCCESS

In order to succeed, you must know what you are doing, like what you are doing and believe in what you are doing.
—Will Rogers, humorist

Success is determined by taking the hand you were dealt and utilizing it to the very best of your ability.
—Ty Boyd

Failure has been correctly identified as the path of least "persistence."

# SUCCESS

The successful family has Work as the father and Integrity as the mother. If you can get along with the parents you won't have any trouble with the rest of the family.

The most practical, beautiful philosophy in the world won't work—if you won't.

People don't plan to fail, they just fail to plan.

# SUCCESS

You cannot climb the ladder of
success with your hands in your
pockets.


We don't pay the price for success,
we pay the price for failure.


By the mile it's a trial; by the
yard it's hard; but by the inch
it's a cinch!

# SUCCESS

Success is dependent upon the glands—sweat glands.

God don't sponsor no flops.
—Ethel Waters,
jazz and blues singer

When you're tough on yourself, life is going to be infinitely easier on you.
—Zig Ziglar

# John Wooden

# SUCCESS

Work is the foundation of all business, the source of all prosperity, and the parent of genius.

The price of success is much lower than the price of failure.

Be more concerned with your character than with your reputation. Your character is what you really are while your reputation is merely what others think you are.

—John Wooden,
NCAA coach

# SUCCESS

Too many people spend more time planning how to get the job than on how to become productive and successful in that job.

It is not the situation, but the way we respond to the situation that's important.

You were born to win, but in order to become a winner you must plan to win and prepare to win. Then you can legitimately expect to win.

# SUCCESS

Success seems to be largely a
matter of hanging on after others
have let go.
—William Feather

Endurance is the crowning quality.
—James Russell Lowell,
poet, editor, essayist and diplomat

Always bear in mind that your own
resolution to succeed is more
important than any other one thing.
—Abraham Lincoln,
16th president of the U.S.

# Woodrow Wilson

# SUCCESS

The successful person is prosperous because he has developed 95 percent of his ability. The failure is poor because only 5 percent of his natural talents have been utilized.

—Charles E. Popplestone

Surely a man has come to himself only when he has found the best that is in him and has satisfied his heart with the highest achievement he is fit for.

—Woodrow Wilson,
28th president of the U.S.

# SUCCESS

The difference between ordinary
and extraordinary is that little extra.

The talent of success is nothing
more than doing what you can
do well, and doing well whatever
you do.

—Henry Wadsworth Longfellow,
poet

Success...seems to be connected
with action. Successful people keep
moving. They make mistakes,
but they don't quit.

—Conrad Hilton,
hotel magnate

If you strive for quality of life first, standard of living invariably goes up; if you seek standard of living first, there is no guarantee that the quality of life will improve.
—Zig Ziglar

Criticize the performance, not the performer.

Make the most of yourself, for that is all there is of you.
—Ralph Waldo Emerson, philosophical essayist, poet and lecturer

Duty makes us do
things well, but love
helps us do them
beautifully.

# RELATIONSHIPS

Life is an echo. What you send out, you get back. What you give, you get.

Do unto others as you would have them do unto you.

It's impossible to influence someone else for the good and give them a boost without gaining a benefit yourself.

# RELATIONSHIPS

You get the best out of others
when you give the best of yourself.
—Harvey Firestone, industrialist

People don't care how much you
know until they know how much
you care—about them.

Successful people use their strength
by recognizing, developing and
utilizing the talents of others.

# RELATIONSHIPS

Personal relationships are the fertile soil from which all advancement, all success, all achievement in real life grows.
—Ben Stein

Be a good-finder—look for the good in others.

You do affect others either for good or for bad—positively or negatively.

# RELATIONSHIPS

You can only see in others what is inside of you.


People pay more attention to what you do than what you say.


Real love is a growing and development process that involves every emotion, problem, joy and triumph known to man.

# RELATIONSHIPS

Before we can properly handle
a problem, we must know all of
the problem.

A lot of people have gone further
than they thought they could
because someone else thought
they could.

There is no such thing as a self-
made man. You will reach your
goals only with the help of others.
—George Shinn

# RELATIONSHIPS

How many marriages would be better if the husband and the wife clearly understood that they're on the same side?

The greatest good we can do for others is not to share our riches with them, but to reveal theirs.

Appreciative words are the most powerful force for good on earth.
—George W. Crane

The more you "pass on" to others,
the more you keep for yourself.

There is no limit to what can be
accomplished when no one cares
who gets the credit.
—John Wooden, NCAA coach

Recipe for having friends:
Be one.
—Elbert Hubbard

# RELATIONSHIPS

The best portion of a good life is
the little nameless, unremembered
acts of kindness and of love.
—William Wordsworth,
English poet

You will find as you look back
upon your life that the moments
that stand out, the moments when
you have really lived, are the
moments when you have done
things in a spirit of love.
—Henry Drummond

It takes so little to make people happy. Just a touch, if we know how to give it, just a word fitly spoken, a slight readjustment of some bolt or pin or bearing in the delicate machinery of a soul.

—Frank Crane

The best thing about giving of ourselves is that what we get is always better than what we give. The reaction is greater than the action.

—Orison Swett Marden

# About the author

Zig Ziglar's enthusiasm, understanding, and ability to communicate with people of all ages have made him one of the most widely read and listened-to motivational teachers in America. His sure-fire formulas for personal improvement have been studied by thousands in their quest for success and have earned him the stature of being one of America's most sought-after speakers.

Zig resides in Dallas, where he is chairman of the multinational training company bearing his name. The Zig Ziglar Corporation, internationally known as "The Training Company," helps spread Zig's message to Corporate America via its many custom-tailored seminars, video and audio programs.

For information on the many products and seminars offered by the Zig Ziglar Corporation, call toll free: 800-527-0306. In Dallas call 214-233-9191.